This book belongs to

Reading Central Library

Rachel
Jane ₓ

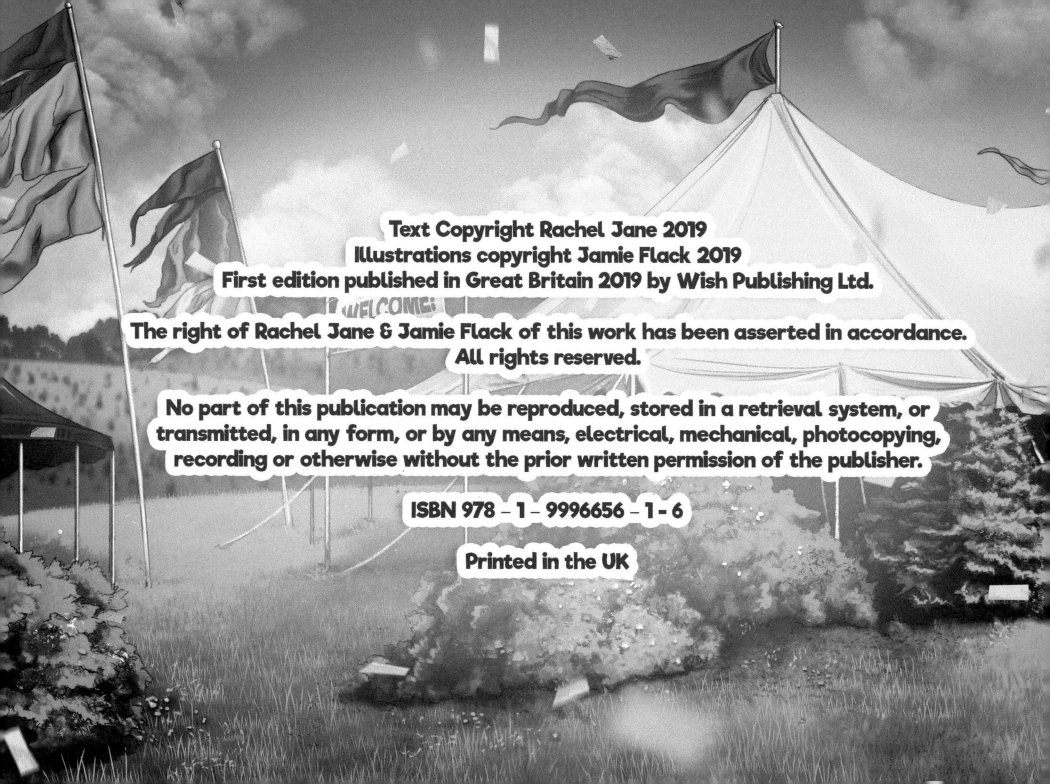

TALLULAH GOES TO THE FESTIVAL

WRITTEN BY RACHEL JANE
ILLUSTRATED BY JAMIE FLACK

At the Festival of Love!

They turn the last corner
And now they arrive
At the Festival of Love
Which is coming alive.

What a day it's been, with all the bands I've seen.
I've had so much fun, singing in the sun,
I've made a new friend and sung until the end...

Of the Festival of Love!